# GROWING UP GRIZZLY

The True Story of Baylee and Her Cubs

# GROWING UP GRIZZLY

Concept and photos by Amy Shapira • Text by Douglas H. Chadwick

**FALCON**GUIDE®

GUILFORD, CONNECTICUT
HELENA, MONTANA
AN IMPRINT OF THE GLOBE PEQUOT PRESS

To buy books in quantity for corporate use
or incentives, call **(800) 962–0973**
or e-mail **premiums@GlobePequot.com.**

FalconGuides is an imprint of Globe Pequot Press.

Falcon and FalconGuides are registered trademarks
of Morris Book Publishing, LLC.

Text design: Martine Traulaugn, Design + Know-How

**The Library of Congress has cataloged the hard-
cover edition as follows:**
Shapira, Amy.
    Growing up grizzly : the true story of Baylee and
    her cubs / concept and photos by Amy Shapira ;
    text by Douglas H. Chadwick.—1st ed.
        p. cm.—(A Falcon guide)
    ISBN-13: 978-0-7627-4149-6
    ISBN-10: 0-7627-4149-X
        1. Grizzly bear—Alaska—Anecdotes. 2. Grizzly
    bear—Alaska—Pictorial works. I. Chadwick,
    Douglas H. II. Title. III. Series.

QL737.C27S475 2007
599.784092'9—dc22

                                        2006005884

ISBN 978-0-7627-7979-6

Printed in the United States of America
First Edition/First Printing

For my husband, Israel, whose love and
generosity of spirit have allowed me to
follow my dreams, and for Baylee, who
lives in the wild yet inhabits my heart.

—A. S.

For my youngest brother, Gordon.

—D. H. C.

In southeastern Alaska, a wild forest grows between the mountains and the sea. In the middle of this forest shines a lake, and on one end of the lake is a cozy, hidden-away cove. More than twenty grizzly bears come here every summer when the cove's fresh waters are full of swimming salmon.

Grizzlies love to catch these silvery fish. Eating lots of salmon is important to keep big bear bellies full and help small bears grow up healthy and strong.

One day out by the ocean's edge, a grizzly bear came walking along a beach. From there, he followed a long river through the forest all the way to the lake. Then he walked around the lake and into the cove.

He traveled by himself the whole time.

The people who watch grizzlies at the cove had never seen this bear before. Nobody knew where he first started his journey or how many days he had been walking. No one knew much about him at all except that he didn't want to travel any farther. He stayed around the cove, and after a while, people started to call this bear Emmett.

Emmett wasn't a little cub. He wasn't a yearling cub either. He was two years old. That's when grizzly bears usually leave home. Emmett was old enough to live on his own. But he didn't seem to want to. Maybe he wasn't sure what to do now that he was away from his old family and the place where he grew up. Sometimes he wore a goofy look on his face. Most of the time, he just looked lost and lonely.

Emmett would play with trees. He found a bucket and played with it.

When Emmett saw his reflection in the window of an old cabin, he played with that too.

This young grizzly really needed a friend.

Other grizzlies were visiting the cove at the same time.

One family of four bears fished and played there nearly every day. People called the mother Baylee. She had three new cubs that people named Eleanor, Misha, and James.

Eleanor, the smallest cub, was quiet and shy.
Her brother James was the biggest cub. He was also the friendliest.

Misha, the middle-size cub, was the busiest and the noisiest. Misha had enough energy for two baby bears. Even when Misha was resting, you could tell from his look that he was ready to do something—like grab onto his toes and roll down a hill, making all kinds of little grizzly grumbles and growls.

Emmett spent hour after hour following Baylee's family around. He stared and stared at her and her three cubs, Eleanor, James, and Misha. Emmett was growing fast, but he wasn't quite ready to be grown-up. What he wanted more than anything else was to join in the family's fun.

Baylee wrestled and tumbled with her cubs. She cuddled them and kept watch to be sure they didn't wander too far. She was one of the gentlest bears in the cove.

But every time Emmett walked near, Baylee would growl and make him go away. Even the nicest mother grizzlies don't like anything or anybody to bother their babies. So whenever the family went somewhere together, all Emmett could do was follow far behind and watch.

And watch some more. And wait and hope, while Baylee's cubs got to explore places and chase ducks and romp in the grass side by side.

Baylee's cubs were too little to catch salmon for themselves. Baylee had to catch fish for them. One afternoon, she left her cubs on the shore and went to her favorite rock to look for salmon in the water below.

She saw a salmon far from the edge and made a great big grizzly bear dive.

She got it!

While she was away, Emmett had come over to where the cubs were waiting for their mother. The three little bears sniffed Emmett and made room for him. Just like that, they became friends. So when Baylee returned, she found four young bears standing together instead of three. Baylee didn't growl or roar. She didn't chase Emmett away. This time she let him stay.

In the days that followed, Baylee brought Emmett fish and let him drink her milk. She played with him just like she played with her cubs. No one ever heard of a mother grizzly doing this before. But every grizzly is a little bit different from every other one. Emmett must have been very glad that this is true. Walking beside Baylee and her cubs, he was a happy-looking bear. He had found a family.

Baylee needed a few more naps than usual. Taking care of four grizzly cubs, including a big one, would make anybody tired once in a while.

Soon it was fall. Most of the salmon left the cove. The grizzlies began moving away into the forest looking for sweet berries and roots to eat. Baylee and her cubs left too. When they traveled among the tall trees and mountainsides, they took Emmett with them, because the lonely bear from far away was part of the family now.

The days turned colder, and before long it was time to spend the winter resting. Baylee dug a den deep into the ground and put soft tree branches on the floor. Emmett snuggled up beside her and the cubs in this bear bedroom while deep snow turned the world outside white and hushed. He had a long, warm, wonderful sleep.

Another summer came. Many of the bears that lived in the forest came back to the cove to fish. Baylee returned to the cove with her family. All of the young bears with her had grown, especially Emmett. His muscles were thicker. His claws were longer. His nose was also getting longer. He could tell about all kinds of things that were going on far away just by smelling the wind, the same as grown-up grizzlies do. Eleanor was still the smallest cub and just a little bit shy. James was still the biggest, friendliest cub.

Misha, the middle-size cub, was still the busiest, ready as always to play or pounce.

Baylee had to catch fish for all of them. She didn't seem to mind, even though Emmett was three years old now and almost as tall as she was.

Some days, Emmett wandered off on his own to explore. He still liked to play with trees. Once in a while, he would get so busy rolling over rocks or digging holes that he forgot where his new family was. As soon as Emmett saw he was alone again, he would start to bawl.

Baylee, the mother with the extra-big heart, would go over to find him. Her cubs would gather around Emmett and make him feel at home once again.

All the cubs and Emmett wrestled with each other. They all wrestled with Baylee, too. Sometimes it looked liked real fighting, but it never was. It was pretend-fighting. Grizzlies like to roughhouse this way. Young bears get to practice using the speed and strength they need to survive in wild places. They also learn how to be careful with their power so they won't hurt any playmates.

No matter how much pretend-fighting they did, everyone in the family took good care of each other and stayed friends all summer long.

When the leaves started to turn autumn colors, the grizzly family of five left the cove to find berries in the forest. They dug tasty roots from the ground while the weather grew frosty and the first snowflakes fell from the clouds. Then, with their tummies full, the bears had another good, long rest in a den. Emmett snuggled in next to Baylee and the cubs just like the winter before.

The next summer, Baylee was one of the first bears to arrive in the cove.
But this year she came without her cubs.

Baylee's cubs were two-year-old bears now. The time had come for them to stop following their mother and begin to live life on their own. Misha was there in another part of the cove, full of his usual energy. He was having no trouble catching salmon by himself.

Eleanor was there. She wasn't small any more. She was turning into such a big grizzly that she was starting to look like her mother. Sometimes Eleanor was by herself and sometimes with her brother Misha.

And sometimes she was with her brother James. James would go diving to get fish like he used to watch his mother do. Then he would shake-shake-shake-shake himself dry.

Finally, there was Emmett, taller and heavier and stronger than ever. He still looked sort of goofy now and then. Sometimes he even looked a little like the two-legged animals called people. But he didn't look worried about being alone anymore.

Emmett was going to leave the cove before long. Maybe he would come back to visit the cove next summer. Or perhaps he would move on to live in another part of the wild Alaskan forest between the mountains and the sea. No one could say for sure. But everybody could tell that Emmett was ready to take his own place in the world and be a grown-up grizzly bear at last, thanks to one kind mother named Baylee and three friendly cubs.

These are all real bears, and this a true story about their lives.
It happened just this way from the beginning to the end.

# A Note from the Photographer

Photographing a grizzly in the wild has always been my dream. In the summer of 2000, I traveled to a remote cove in the Alaskan wilderness. Glacial waters tumbled down from roaring waterfalls and filled the tiny inlet. Snow-capped mountains, towering hemlock, and Sitka spruce surrounded the cove. It was in this setting of rugged splendor that I took my first grizzly bear photograph and found a new consciousness and commitment to my life.

My dream became my passion; the bears and their habitat my sanctuary. Each summer since, I have spent my days photographing Baylee and Mona (the two female adults who are full-time summer residents), their cubs, and their adolescent offspring. I have come to know the bears as charming, fierce, loving, intense, comical, highly intelligent, and always majestic. I have returned year after year to be in the presence of their wild, untamed spirit.

In the summer of 2002, Baylee (named in honor of a wildlife biologist's eldest daughter) and her three cubs made their first appearance. As it was my third trip to the cove, I had come to expect the unexpected. Yet I was still amazed by Baylee. She is a very unusual grizzly, and her adoption of Emmett (named by a local guide) quite remarkable. I spent the next three summers under the spell of this mother bear, her three natural cubs, and her equally captivating adopted son. It was a rare opportunity.

In the summer of 2005, Baylee appeared with her two new cubs (see the following pages). She was as good-hearted and nurturing as ever. James, Misha, and Eleanor remained nearby. At times they played together, but most often they stayed apart. Baylee had taught them well, and they were thriving. Emmett, now an adult grizzly, had left the cove to venture out into the world.

Wanting to share these events with others, I turned to Douglas Chadwick—naturalist, prolific author, and friend. Doug's words and my images tell the story exactly as it unfolded. My hope is that children and adults of all ages will enjoy this story of a most unusual grizzly bear family.

Amy Shapira
January 2006

Photographer **Amy Shapira** returned to the same remote cove in the Alaskan wilderness for six consecutive summer amassing more than 7,500 images for this book. Several of her photographs have been featured on a PBS documentary and many have been published in magazines and newspapers. Amy is deeply dedicated to the protecton, restoration, and conservation of North America's grizzly habitat. She lives in Carbondale, Colorado, with her husband Israel and their three dogs.

**Douglas H. Chadwick** is a biologist who has studied animals around the world. He had written nine books and hundreds of articles about nature for popular magazines such as *National Geographic*. Fascinated by grizzly bears for most of his grown-up life, Douglas and his wife reared two children in a remote cabin on the edge of Glacier Park, and had grizzlies for close neighbors for years. Today Doug still lives close to bears in Whitefish, Montana.

The authors pledge to donate a portion of the proceeds
from the sale of this book to Vital Ground.

Vital Ground, a nonprofit conservation organization, works with private landowners to protect essential habitat in the last ecosystems where grizzlies roam. Together with its many partners, the group has helped conserve more that a quarter of a million acres in Alaska and the heart of the Rocky Mountains. For more information visit www.vitalground.org.